D0536953

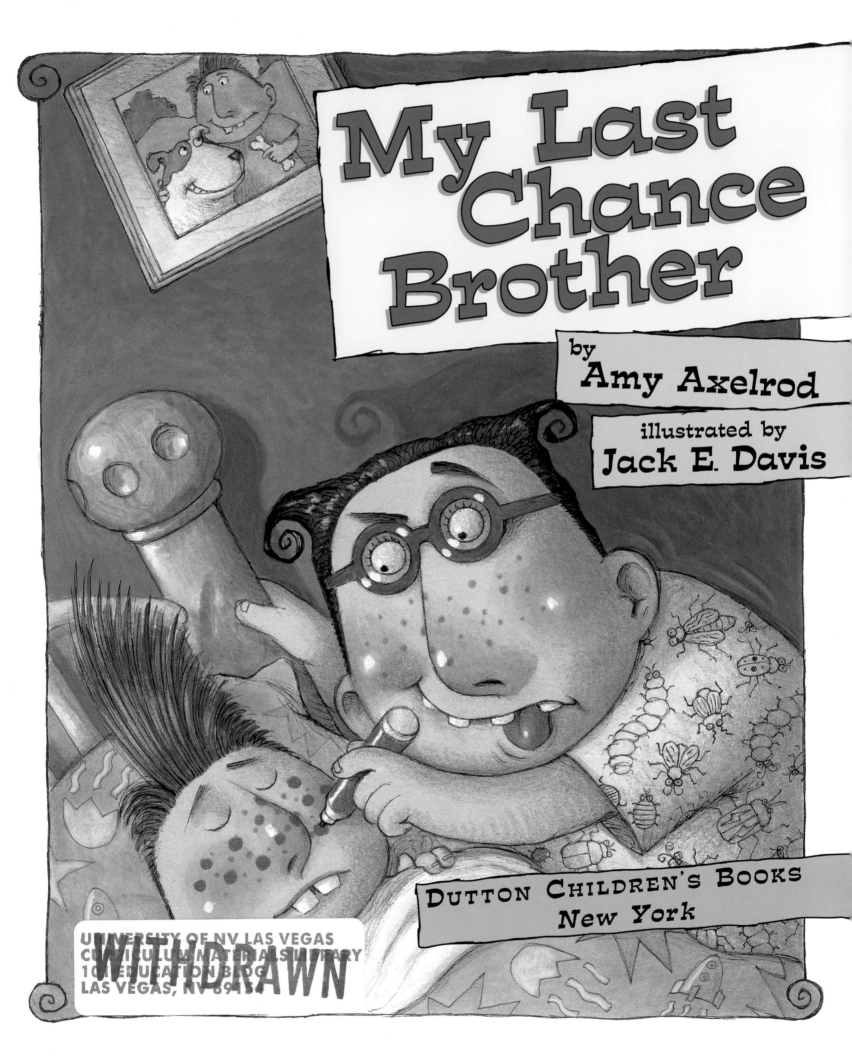

My Last Chance Brother

by
Amy Axelrod

illustrated by
Jack E. Davis

DUTTON CHILDREN'S BOOKS
New York

UNIVERSITY OF NV LAS VEGAS
CURRICULUM MATERIALS LIBRARY
101 EDUCATION BLDG
LAS VEGAS, NV 89154

WITHDRAWN

Text copyright © 2002 by Amy Axelrod

Illustrations copyright © 2002 by Jack E. Davis

All rights reserved.

CIP Data is available.

Published in the United States 2002 by Dutton Children's Books,

a division of Penguin Putnam Books for Young Readers

345 Hudson Street, New York, New York 10014

www.penguinputnam.com

Typography by Richard Amari

Printed in Hong Kong

First Edition

1 3 5 7 9 10 8 6 4 2

ISBN 0-525-46659-2

For Mark David Snyder,
my last chance brother,
and for siblings everywhere
A.A.

For Baby Ben.
J.E.D.

That guy with his finger in my cake is my brother, Gordon.

But only until tomorrow.

In the morning, if I get my wish, he's going to wake up as **BUG BOY**.

That's because this morning, when I was fast asleep, he snuck into my room and rubbed my head till it hurt.

"SURPRISE!" he yelled. "Gotta activate those brain cells for your birthday, Max!"

BAM!!

Today, after breakfast, when his boring best friend came over, Gordon **SLAMMED** his bedroom door right in my face, so I had to listen really hard.

But later, when my friends came over, he walked right into my room, like he owned it. Everybody was so busy watching his dumb magic trick that no one even looked at my new spaceship.

I never should've told him I was afraid of spiders. When I opened his present, the kids laughed so hard that soda came out of their noses.

Let's see how he likes it when all his legs get stuck on the **flypaper** I'll put up on his walls. **I'LL** be the one laughing then.

For dinner tonight we went to my favorite Chinese restaurant. When my parents weren't looking, Gordon stuck some chopsticks in my ears. Then he cracked open my fortune cookie and read it out loud. "Beware of eating yellow snow," he said. I believed him—until everyone at the next table started to laugh.

But that's okay. When he's got antennae and a **shell**, he won't be allowed in any restaurants.

Mom says that deep down Gordon loves me, and I should give him one more chance.

Why should I?

He grabs the comics first every day.

He **NEVER** slows down on his bike.

He pins me down and tries to **drool** on me.

He drops my toothbrush in the toilet and says it was an accident.
He calls me a girl.
And the worst thing is... he **breathes** on me.

But I'll get even.
I'll put him under glass
and charge all of his
friends money to see him.
I'll be RICH, and he'll
just bUZZ.

I can't wait until tomorrow morning, when he's **BUG BOY**.

"My services, free of charge!"

"Thanks," I force myself to tell him.

"You want me to stay with you for a while?" Gordon asks.

"Okay," I say, just to make him feel better.

"Move over," he says.

"Just one thing," I say to him.

"What's that?" he asks.

"Breathe in the other direction."

Maybe Mom's right. Maybe I'll give him one last chance. I'm pretty sure my fingers were crossed when I made that wish. 'Cause you never know...

That spider could've had brothers.